How to Be Friends with a BOY

How to Be Friends with a

How to Be Friends with a BOY

How to Be Friends with a

Judi Miller

SCHOLASTIC INC.
New York Toronto London Auckland Sydney

ISBN 0-590-42806-3

 Published by Scholastic Inc.

12 11 10 9 8 7 6 5 4 3 2 1 0 1 2 3 4 5/9

Printed in the U.S.A. 01

First Scholastic printing, October 1990

For:

Beth Mencher
Jessica Hernandez
Heather Garber
Darcie Goetz
Raven Bunch
Elayne Streity
Mandeep Jassal
Richard Robben
Alexander Saingchin
Christina Frankel
David Gutierrez
Matthew Hefferman
Inmay Kiely
Kenya Nevith

and all the other children who talked to me about making friendships, whether boy or girl.

CONTENTS

How to Be Friends with a BOY

How to Be Friends with a

Introduction

MANY of the girls and boys who talked to me during the writing of this book automatically assumed we were talking about boys who have crushes on girls, or girls who "kind of" like boys in their classes.

But there's a BIG difference between being attracted to someone and becoming spell-bound, afraid to speak to them, and having girlFRIENDS and boyFRIENDS who are fun, and with whom you can hang out and talk to.

Some girls and boys did feel that having same-sex friendships got a little flat or down-right boring. But some of those girls and boys found their same-sex friends didn't agree, and so they had to fight to have a girlFRIEND or boyFRIEND.

What Are Girls Really Like?
What Are Boys Really Like?

What I did was talk to many different girls and boys. Then I took those who were similar, and combined them into characters. The characters are *real* but made up. See if you can find yourself or your friends in any of the characters. Then as you read the book and Alison or Richie speaks, flip back to their whole characterization if you have to.

Many of them want to have friends just like you. Many of them are ready to have a boyFRIEND or a girlFRIEND just like you. Throughout the book there will be quizzes and questions to answer to give you further insight.

Don't limit yourself to reading the boys' section if you are a boy or reading the girls' section if you are a girl. At least skim the other side to gain more information. In fact, read the whole book.

But first we need to define: What is friendship?

Think about it. Then ask yourself: What *isn't* friendship? Friendship is *not* trying to appear cool, finding it hard to swallow, not knowing what to do or say. That is "liking" someone.

Now think of that *crush* becoming a friend

and see what happens. You can talk, you don't feel like you have peanut butter stuck to the roof of your mouth, and you can have fun. You can share your joys with this friend. You can even tell him or her your problems. But the difference is this friend is not exactly like you.

You can find out all about boys if you're a girl.

You can find out all about girls if you're a boy.

It's a special friendship and should be handled like one. Then, later in life, say around ninth grade, you can combine a very special friendship with a boy or girl you also "like." And it may even be the same special friend you have now!

Cast of Characters

Richie — The tallest boy in his sixth-grade class, he could pass for an eighth-grader in the halls. He has chestnut-colored hair. One girl said he is quiet, almost shy. He doesn't want to get too close to anyone because he thinks he might get hurt. But outwardly he is fun; he makes jokes and everyone wants to be near him. His parents are divorced, and he's close with both his mother and his dad. Richie reminds some girls of the cartoon character L'il Abner.

Alison — She is the shortest girl in the class, with shiny reddish-blonde hair that frames her heart-shaped face. She's on her turf with many girlfriends; she was a Brownie and is now in the Girl Scouts. She doesn't know how to have a boyFRIEND yet, but while she's waiting to find out she gives good advice. She wears Coca-Cola socks with red-and-black stripes.

Joey — Voted The Boy Most Likely to Get Into Trouble Before the Sixth Grade, lively Joey likes girls. He has blond curly hair and clear blue eyes and is short and skinny. He is also the class clown. When the teacher's back is turned he gets up and does pantomimed imitations of her. As soon as she turns around he is sitting down, looking like an angel, and the whole class is giggling behind their hands. Very popular, Joey looks forward to the chance of having some friends — some really true-blue friends — who are girls.

Beth — In the fifth grade Beth, or Beth-y, has short curly black hair and violet eyes. She was a boy-hater because of the obnoxious boys in her old school, but she's willing to change. Mainly, she just wants friends. There are two boys in her Sunday school class she "likes" — so she can't talk to them. But in her homeroom at school she is developing two friendships with boys. She just walks up and says, "Hi, want to talk?"

Jeremy — The most popular boy in the sixth grade, tall, dark, and handsome Jeremy has no girlfriends. Funny, a lot of girls "like" him, but they're not fun friends with whom he can talk. With dark brown, straight hair and big brown velvety eyes, Jeremy has an easygoing personality and is everyone's favorite. Both girls and boys like him.

Jessica — She has shiny, dark brown hair — so long that she can sit on it. With her pert nose and wide smile, Jessica is easily the prettiest girl in her sixth-grade class. A lot of boys "like" her, but when she talks to them they clam up and it looks as if they don't like her at all. Jessica wears red a lot, which is her favorite color, so you can't miss her. She wants to have friends who are boys. She thinks it would be fun.

Eric — Short, kind of roly-poly, with reddish-blond hair that falls in his face, Eric is always smiling or chuckling about something. Voted "Funniest" in the fifth grade "secret" slam book, he makes people laugh without even trying. You would think Eric has a lot of girlfriends as well as boyfriends. Actually, having no sisters, Eric is shy around girls and wishes one would break the ice.

Debbie — As pretty as she is smart, Deborah misses the boat with the boys in her sixth-grade class. Though she would like to be friends with boys, she's begun to think it's not possible because they just don't talk to her. Impatient, she wants to take drastic measures. Right now, despite her cute clothes and her hair up in brightly colored ribbons, Debbie thinks boys are as colorful as mud.

Other Characters

Lauren — Sixth grade. Popular. Hates boys.

Mitchell — Fifth grade. Shy. Afraid of Girls.

Robyn — Fifth grade. Reluctant to be included in Cast of Characters. Waits for boys to come to her.

Roger — Sixth grade. Waiting to make his move. Thinks friendships with girls would be fun.

We've even pulled in an expert. Meet Bambi Levine, who's in the eighth grade, writes for the school paper, and wants to make it big, just like Dear Abby and Dear Ann. Here she is, our own Dear Bambi:

Dear Bambi,
They say I'm too young for boys, too old for dolls. What can I do?

Signed,
In-between

Dear In-between,
Don't throw out your Barbies yet. And Prince Charming may come in the form of someone who has a mad, passionate urge to play punchball with you

— Bambi

Dear Bambi,
I am in the sixth grade. I formerly thought girls were unnecessary. Then I met this new girl on my block, and she and I play basketball in her yard. It isn't that I don't like her — I

do. But I never felt anything like this. We can even talk about our problems.

Signed,
Never Felt

Dear Never Felt,

I know you never felt, but now you do. Nice, isn't it?

— Bambi

Dear Bambi,

Yesterday the boy who sits behind me tapped me on the shoulder and said he liked my dress. He hasn't spoken to me since school began. I thought he hated me. And here I kind of like him or at least I think he's cute. What should I do to get him to be a boyFRIEND?

Signed,
Now What

Dear Now What,

You know what? Just read this book and let it help you make lots of new friendships!

— Bambi

How to Be Friends with a
BOY

1.
Friends, Friends, You Can Never Have Too Many Friends!

DEBBIE says passionately:

> *"Agghhh! Oh, you've got to be kidding! Friends with a boy? That's like stepping onto the Planet of the Apes and calling a truce. You've got to be joking! Say that you're joking. Anyone who wants to be friends with a boy* must *be joking. The idea is ahead of its time."*

Lauren has this to say:

> *"That'll be the day. You mean — being* friends *with a boy? That's funny when you think about it."*

Robyn is waiting:

"Someday some boy will come up and ask me to play kickball with him after school. I think it could happen. I hope it's with a boy that I 'like.' "

Alison thinks it could work:

"I've been thinking about this for a long time, being friends with boys. If I had lessons maybe I could do it. Like I have ballet lessons. Can someone teach that?

"But first of all, it would flip out all the girls in my club. Second of all, I don't care. Third of all, I don't think *I care."*

What do the boys think?
Richie says:

"Friends with girls! That's impossible. Not good *friends. How are you supposed to be friends with girls?"*

Jeremy and Joey think alike:

"It's not possible. It wouldn't work. How could it possibly work? Could it work?"

Jeremy says casually:

"You know, I like girls but they don't talk or laugh. They're not a lot of fun like boys."

If you've been keeping up with the Cast of Characters you know that Jeremy is the most popular boy in the sixth grade and every girl has a crush on him. Consequently, they're all afraid to talk to him. He thinks girls aren't fun. As Beth says in her diary:

Dear Diary,
This morning I sat next to Jeremy in assembly. I couldn't talk to him. I couldn't even think of what to say. Our elbows touched and I'm sure he likes me. Maybe he's shy, too?

Are you beginning to see the difference between "liking" and liking a boy? If you were *friends*, that all-too-familiar robotlike feeling would vanish. Why? Because you wouldn't have a crush on him, that's why. You could talk, laugh, make jokes with, disagree with, tell your problems to a *boy!*

Think about it. It's your chance to figure out if girls aren't at least a little like boys.

Singing the Clubhouse Blues?

Are you in a club like the NBC's or the ABC's

or the CBS's or the Jaguars or the Jasmines? Girls in your club may not want you to have a boyFRIEND. Especially if *they* don't. Boys may be the enemy.

Well, what can you do? Stay in the club and drop your new fun boyFRIEND? Keep your boyFRIEND and be kicked out of your club and exiled by all your girlfriends? It's a terrible choice to make. If you want to have girlfriends and keep your new kind of friendship, you may have to get every girl in your club a boy-FRIEND!

What you are experiencing is PEER PRESSURE. And when peer pressure raises its ugly head — watch out. It happens to just about everyone.

Eric says:

"Well, it's not going to happen to me because I don't have any girlFRIENDS. I'm not in any boys' clubs, either. I'm free of all that peer pressure."

What is peer pressure? Well, your friends are your peers — your equals — and that's what makes you friends. But they put pressure on you to *stay* equal. If you're sporting a new-found boyFRIEND or two, they're not going to like it.

As Jessica says:

"I was starting to be friendly with this guy on my block. Every day we played on his block with his friends. My girlfriends took a vote that if I didn't play with them, *I would be excluded from their friendship. EXCLUDED FROM THEIR FRIENDSHIP. I didn't even know what that meant!"*

Most of the girls I talked to were even afraid to admit that though they had boyFRIENDS, they also had problems having the relationship, problems that came from the group of girls they were friendly with. Most solved these problems by spending equal time with their boyFRIENDS and girlfriends.

Q: How do you stop peer pressure?
A: You can't.

Here is a story to tuck into your memory bank. It's from Beth.

"It all started this summer. I met him when I went with my mother to her friend's house. It

was agreed by both of us that we would pretend we were having a good time when he didn't like girls and I didn't know much about boys. We had so much fun that we became friends. I don't know how it happened. Mostly we talked and then we found we both liked to play punchball.

"But then he moved away. He lived on the other side of town and you could only get there by car. We never talked on the telephone.

"So after that we became pen pals.

"But what I remember most about that friendship, which seemed so nice at the time, was my girlfriends trying to talk me out of it. I wasn't even cutting into their time but they didn't like it and that was enough.

"It didn't make sense. I asked Duke — that's his name — if his boyfriends didn't like the fact that we played punchball together and went for long walks and went swimming in his next-door neighbor's pool. He said they didn't like it. None of the guys he hung around with had a girl for a friend. It would take time away from their sports.

"So I know all about peer pressure, only that summer I called it 'the green-eyed monster — JEALOUSY.' "

Peer pressure can tear you apart, as if you were being pulled one way by a team of girls, and another way by one lone boy. What can you do?

1. **Explain** — Just explain to the girls that you haven't stopped being their friend, but you want to split your time between them and your new friendship. Assure them that they'll still get most of your time. That's fair, isn't it?

2. **Explain again** — Explain to your new boyFRIEND that the new friendship has made your other friends antsy, concerned that they're going to lose something in the deal.

It is true that many of the girls may be envious of the ease with which you're able to have a friend who's a boy. Some might even confuse it with a BOYfriend. While you're just having fun climbing trees with Mikey, they may think you're the only one in the fifth grade to have a BOYfriend. This is because lots of girls don't know the difference.

Which brings us to Number 3.

3. **Be clear** — that this boy is a *friend*. That you have no intention of ignoring your girlfriends. That this boy is also your friend and you want to spend time with him, too.

One girl said that the best solution was not

to spend too much time with your boy-FRIEND. Though it is fun to have a boy-FRIEND, peer pressure can make it hard. Most of the girls I talked to said, "Yes, well, there's always that."

2.
The How To's

MOST friendships with boys are made in school, where boys and girls can spend some time together at recess or at free time participating in activities or playing in groups. You have to work at anything you want, and the same goes for a friendship with a boy.

1. **Talk** — Alison advises:

"Listen, I can't carry on a relationship with a boy who won't talk. I had one like that, and I couldn't stand those creepy pauses. It was too much work."

It goes without saying that the boy you pick to be your special friend already knows how to talk, and you talk to each other a lot. That's one thing you shouldn't have to work on. Just work on picking the right boy.

2. **Listen** — Richie says:

"For me to like a girl at all she has to be a good talker. Girls are like that. They're good at talking."

Robyn says:

"Whoa, now wait a second! Girls aren't just wind-up talking robots. Half of the responsibility should be with the boy."

Some of the best "talking" you can do is listening. Encourage your boyFRIEND to do some of the talking, and you listen. Listening means not interrupting, not changing the subject, really *listening*. And not just listening but hearing what he's saying, and responding.

3. **Be yourself** — The obvious comeback is: "Well, who did you expect me to be?"

But, we're not talking about the stiff, unresponsive, scared you that takes over when your crush passes by. Maybe you smile — or maybe you *think* you're smiling — but you aren't having the conversation you would have if your crush was your chum.

Beth thinks the whole thing gets to be funny. She reveals a universal truth for girls and boys and even adults who probably know better. As she says:

> *"When I'm not myself, I start acting 'cool.' I'm Ms. Cool around the boys I like but that isn't how I really feel. Inside I feel like a stranger took over my body and kicked me out. Everything I say comes out in this voice that sounds stuck-up, even to me."*

It's important to everybody to be cool in the fifth and sixth grades. But it's one thing to be cool and in control, and another thing to be cool and unfriendly.

To recap:

Talk.

Listen.

Be yourself.

Making Time for Boys

It takes time to be a girlFRIEND. And, as we discussed before, peer pressure can make it hard to spend *any* time with a boy. Most girls meet their boyFRIENDS in the school yard at recess, or during free time at school. If your boyFRIEND lives on your block, you might want to play after school or have him over to your house for dinner.

As Jessica puts it:

"On Monday I have ballet. On Tuesday I have drama class. On Wednesday I have tap. On Thursday I have baton twirling. On Friday I have my piano lesson. On Saturday morning I have my Girl Scout meeting. I hardly have time for my girlfriends!"

Perhaps Jessica wouldn't have to alter her schedule at all. Maybe she could play with her special friend at school, in the school yard. But then, of course, her girlfriends would see she had a special friend she was paying attention to, instead of hanging out with them.

And there you are, back to peer pressure.

Finish this chapter by taking this simple true-false test:

1. I'm very popular with boys and don't need to read all this stuff.

2. I talk at the drop of a hat.

3. I always talk to everyone. Even on a bus. Talking comes naturally to me.

4. I always listen, too. Try me.

5. I have plenty of good friends who are boys.

6. I have friends at school who are boys.
7. I have friends on my block who are boys.
8. I am never shy.
9. I am way ahead of the boys in my class.
10. I have nothing to learn.

Each time you answered "true" give yourself ten points. If your score is 100, great! But remember, you can never have too many friends. If your score is 50–90, you're on the right track! And if your score is less than 50, don't lose hope. You'll soon have lots of friends — girls *and* boys! No matter what your score is: Read on!

3.
The Perfect BoyFRIENDSHIP — Pen Pals!

It's perfect! He doesn't talk. He writes. He introduces himself and you write questions. And you exchange pictures. Opportunity to see what boys are like . . . in another state . . . in another country.

Alison writes to a boy in the fifth grade in London, England, and says:

"He's really neat. His name is Charles, just like the Prince. Once he saw Prince Charles and Princess Di close up, and their children, and he wrote me all about it. I know also that he's shy around the girls in his school and he wants to meet me in person. It kind of broke the ice for me in wanting to be friends with boys."

Jessica has a pen pal in Montmartre, a section of Paris.

"His name is Jean-Pierre. He's my age and he writes to me and I write him back about twice a month. I told him about playing punchball with my friends and he says in the école *where he goes they don't have that game but they play other games. He has a crush on a girl named Yvette, who happens to look just like me. Wouldn't it be funny if we ever met?"*

Even some of the boys have had pen pals who are girls, or they'd like to have one.

Roger had a girl pen pal who lived in Alaska. He thinks she may be the reason that he wants to have friends who are girls. Roger says:

"Hey, it was great. I got to know a girl really well. My handwriting is bad, too, so it improved a lot. But the thing is, it was fun to know a girl. She was athletic — she played soccer and she swam. She was pretty, too. She sent me a picture of her with her brothers after they had all gone fishing and caught a huge fish. It made me want to go to Alaska and meet her. I don't know what happened. Either she got busy or I

got busy, but we stopped writing. I would sure like a girlFRIEND like her."

How do you get a pen pal? Suggest it to your teacher. He or she may start a pen pal club, so that everyone can write. If someone you know has a pen pal, see if you can share that pen pal and write to him. Or, start your own pen pal club. Think of it — no shyness, no exerting yourself, and best of all, you'll get mail! Having a pen pal may be the first step for you having a boyFRIEND.

Where the Boys Are

Where are the boys? Everywhere! That shy fourth-grader you knew may have grown into a friendly fifth-grader. Your boyFRIEND may be sitting right behind you in science. What about next door? Or in your church or synagogue? Or at summer camp? You can meet one at a piano recital. How about a friend of your brother? You and your girlfriends could tick off many, many more ideas.

After you realize that boys are all around you — in the classroom, in the school yard, on your block, at a party your mother makes you go to — you will realize just how easy it is to find a boyFRIEND.

Now What Do You Do?

Why not take some advice from the boys who also want girlFRIENDS and know how to make the *approach*.

Eric says breezily:

"Nothing to it. Just walk up to a boy and say: 'I want to be your friend.' That's one version. Or: 'Can I be your friend?' Well, come to think of it, that doesn't come off right. How about: 'Hey, let's be friends, what do you say?' "

Jessica disagrees:

"No, no. That won't do. A girl should just hang out with boys and girls. Then things will happen naturally. She'll just have a boyFRIEND. Someone will stand out."

Roger comments:

"Yeah, the best way is to just hang out, but then you might get lost in the crowd."

Richie says:

"See, the thing is, I'm mainly hanging out with boys right now. A girl might make a move of

friendship toward me, and I might be cool, but that's not because I don't think she's cute and popular and smart; it's because I don't think I am. So then she gets this kind of rejection."

And then he adds:

"Well, don't blame it on me. That's the way boys are."

Girls, you see what you are up against. *Boys*. Eric has one more thing to include:

"I think to get a boy to notice her, a girl should put a goldfish in his pocket."

All the girls and some of the boys thought that suggestion was a little off the track and gross. But one girl said she might try it.

How to Know Whom to Pick

There's a special type of boy waiting out there to be your boyFRIEND. One clue is: There's an attraction. It's not the same heart-pounding attraction you have with your crush. It's a comfortable feeling, as if you were in your family room at home, sprawled across the floor, watching TV with your girlfriends.

In other words, your boyFRIEND fits the description: comfortable to be with. If he didn't, you wouldn't want to be with him.

Take this true-false quiz and see if a boy you know could be your boyFRIEND.

1. When the bell rings, we usually walk out together and talk until the games start up in the school yard. Usually we play punchball together.

2. It's easy to tell him my problems. The answers I get back are not like my girlfriends' answers.

3. He talks about things naturally. It's easy for him to tell his problems to me.

4. He never gives away a secret of mine.

5. It's hard to explain, but I don't LIKE him, I just like him, and it's nice.

Face it, if you didn't say "true" to each and every statement, you are not enjoying a special friendship with a boyFRIEND. And if you are not, don't you wish you were?

Push aside all ideas of having a *crush*. If you choose a boy you have a crush on, he won't be your friend, anyway. You know you won't be able to talk to him beyond a squeak, and he won't be able to talk to you, either.

Your boyFRIEND:

May be new to the school.

He may have more than one girlFRIEND and you won't care at all.

When you're down and out about some problem he cheers you up.

When he's down and out you have the ability to cheer him up.

When you see him you smile.

You don't care if he's good-looking — he's just so nice to have for a friend.

He's different from your girlfriends. He tells the truth immediately. He doesn't always talk about the same things. He seems nicer somehow.

He's easy to talk to — for a boy.

It's better than having a crush or "liking" a boy. It's a much better feeling.

You don't know how you managed without a boyFRIEND in the first place.

Who Me? Have a Boy for a Friend?

Yes, we know. In the fourth grade you hated all the boys. They were *impossible*. In the third grade you were learning to make girlfriends and in the second grade and first grade everyone was the same and the whole class came to your birthday parties. Boys and girls were more alike. And then as you grew older you grew more apart and were DIFFERENT somehow.

Beth says:

"There's nothing to puzzle over. When I was in fourth grade I hated boys. Now I want to be friends with some. I just walk right up and say, 'Listen, want to be friends?' And then we shake hands."

But what Beth is leaving out is she has carefully researched which boy to pick. The ones who make fun of girls in the hall are out. The ones who made fun of her in the fourth grade are pretty much out, except for a certain few she's undecided about. But you only need a few boyFRIENDS, and Beth is making sure she gets them.

Jeremy, the most popular boy in the sixth grade, has this to reveal:

"I think I like some of my girlFRIENDS better than my buddies. You can't have too many. I wish more girls would approach me and say they wanted to be friends. Girls make great friends. I never thought I could do this, but I can talk about anything with them."

Debbie disagrees:

"See, right away he is wrong. Why should girls approach him? Why doesn't he go after girl-FRIENDS? I think it's a scam!"

Mitchell disagrees with Debbie:

"I don't think it's so bad that Jeremy wants girls to approach him. Boys are shyer than girls. Everyone knows that. It's more natural for girls to make the first move. I wish someone would do it to me."

Robyn disagrees with Mitchell:

"I had a boy come up to me in the fifth grade, extend his hand, and say, 'Hey, do you want to be friends?' We shook hands on it, and we've been friends for about a month."

What do you think?

Ask yourself these questions:

Do I really hate boys as much as I said I did?

Has my life changed since he decided to become my friend?

Do I wish more of my girlfriends had boys

for friends? Then maybe they wouldn't be jealous.

Everything You Always Wanted to Know About Boys but Were Afraid to Ask

Boys know how to listen. They really do.

Boys like to give advice. But watch it if they give too much unasked-for advice.

He's not your BOYFRIEND but he makes you feel special.

Have you always wanted to know everything about boys?

If you just ask them, they'll tell you.

4.
Fear of Rejection

SOONER or later the fear of rejection must come up. It's that fear that when you approach a boy, extend your hand, and say, "Listen, let's be friends," he says, "No, no, a thousand times *no*. I can't stand girls, and more than that, I can't stand *you*."

Can you imagine that happening?

It's more likely that you might make a mistake in choosing the boy. He shakes hands on the "yes" and turns out to be a dud as a friend. He doesn't talk to you, he can't do anything right — he's too shy to pull it off.

Debbie chickens out:

> *"I can't do it. The asking. The boy would have to ask me or someone would have to ask him if he liked me as a friend."*

Jessica says:

"I think a yes or no answer would be a big help here. I really do. I don't think he has to draw her a picture or spell it out. I think he should just say, 'That sounds great' or 'I can't handle it right now.' "

Lauren says:

"It seems like a set-up for failure to me."

But when you think about it, it's awfully hard to reject an offer of friendship. It would be different if you shook hands on being GIRLFRIEND and BOYFRIEND, which hardly ever happens, anyway. Instead of worrying about it, why not plunge right in?

An Ancient Saying

Along with the age-old fear of rejection comes an age-old saying. No one's really proven it to be right, but here it is:

GIRLS MATURE TWO YEARS
FASTER THAN BOYS

Great. Now what do you do? You don't have

class with seventh- or eighth-graders. They probably even go to a different school.

Richie says:

"I never heard that one before. I think it was written by someone who hates boys. I can think of a lot of times girls acted much younger. Boys make them crazy. They're afraid of everything. They cry at the drop of a hat. Nope, I don't believe it."

Robyn remarks:

"You know, I think that means emotionally. Girls are *more mature than boys. I think it starts somewhere in the middle of the third grade or in the beginning of the fourth."*

Alison thinks the saying is ancient:

"I think that was from my mom and dad's time or, come to think of it, my grandparents' time, you know? It seems old-fashioned, doesn't it? Still, I think in some ways it's true."

Beth says:

"I definitely think it's true for some boys and not true for other boys."

For those who want to hang on to the age-old saying because it gives them an edge, they can. But the overall view of the kids interviewed is SO WHAT!

Now that we've covered these two bugaboos we can look at the fear underlying them: SHYNESS.

Why Be Shy?

Alison says:

"I'm shy in large groups, but I could call up a boy, and I can deal with rejection. Certain situations make me shy."

Eric admits without wisecracking:

"Listen, I know I'm a John Candy lookalike but I'm really so shy that if she came up and asked me a flat-out question I would have to make a joke out of it."

Did you hear that, girls? That class clown

who has a smart answer and a joke ready for everybody might just be shy!

Jeremy says:

"I like girls who are spunky, who take the lead. In that way I guess I am shy. I can't start things."

Listen up, girls! He may be the most popular boy in your class, but people come to *him*. And if you come to him with an offer of friendship, then no doubt your new friend will say yes.

Jessica has to deal with boys' shyness:

"I would like to be friends with about half the boys in my class but they're all too shy to talk to me. At first I thought they didn't like me but then I found out they were too shy."

Mitchell is shy and admits it:

"It's not that I'm shy so much, it's that I can't find anything to say when I'm around girls. Everything I say seems wrong. My voice breaks and it gets real high. I guess I'm shy."

Debbie asserts:

"I am not shy. Maybe boys are shy. There has to be a reason they're so boring. That must be it!"

Of course there's shy and then there's *shy*. Most people aren't shy all the time. What they have is called *situational* shyness — they're shy only in certain situations. Boys might be shy or clam up only in front of girls. Girls might feel the same way around boys. Certain situations in school might make you feel shy: gym class, performing in a school play (although that might be stage fright, which feels like an overdose of shyness), a party in school or after school. So these situations make you feel shy when you aren't really shy.

Are there situations where you are shy as compared to always being shy? Maybe in these situations you shouldn't ask someone to become your boyFRIEND. Here are several examples:

Before a spelling bee.

Backstage at your class Christmas pageant.

Before gym class when a big game is planned.

Before the winners of the class elections are announced.

When your mother is coming to school for a PTA event.

But what if you're not *situationally* shy? What if you're shy all the time? Then what? Should you give up? What if it isn't the *situation* but the whole picture?

5.
How to Cope with Your Shyness (Also Known as "Will I Live to See the Seventh Grade?")

NOTICE no one said you had to get rid of your shyness. But how can you cope with it? Why is it there?

A Short Stop for Stutterers

Do you ever stutter? Do you know someone who stutters? Does anyone in your family stutter? Who knows, maybe your boyFRIEND tends to stutter sometimes. How do you act? You should listen very carefully and not make fun of him. You should talk about it only if he does. Some people who stutter are often teased, but that's unfair. Stuttering may be temporary. Stuttering may happen when a person is tired or nervous.

If you stutter, don't let it make you shy. Just remember to finish your sentence and keep talking, no matter how embarrassed you are. It probably doesn't sound as bad as you think.

Heavy-Duty Shyness

In Chapter 9 the boys complain about clamming up. They become so shy that they can't talk, or they blurt out silly things that don't fit.

Are you shy and do you suffer through the Peanut Butter Syndrome? Do you ever feel your tongue is stuck to the roof of your mouth, almost like you've eaten peanut butter? How many other girls feel that way?

Debbie says:

> *"Now that you mention it, I didn't know they had a name for it. Try and talk to a fifth-grade boy and he'll drive you nuts."*

Jessica fesses up:

> *"All I need is jelly. I have the Peanut Butter Syndrome a lot and I get stuck. It's very hard to talk to boys. Especially the boys I know."*

Now that you mention it, that would be understandable if she were trying to talk to a boy she had a hopeless crush on. But again, we're not talking about boys like that. We're talking about making *friends* with a boy. And those kinds of boys shouldn't cause Peanut Butter Syndrome. You should just talk to them like you do to your girlfriends.

So if you're in a situation where you feel hopelessly shy, think over the reason for having boyFRIENDS as opposed to boyfriends. If you have a crush you probably *will* have the Peanut Butter Syndrome, but if you have a friend you'll be able to talk easily. About anything you want.

More About Heavy-Duty Shyness

If you're really, really shy, shy around everyone, you might feel shy around a boyFRIEND. But you will be less shy than you would be around a crush, or around a teacher. Heavy-duty shyness never really goes away. But you must never punish yourself for being shy. That just makes it worse. Chances are you can pick a somewhat shy boyFRIEND.

Richie has some help to give:

"I don't think a girl should feel bad about being shy. Boys feel shy, too, sometimes. I never knew what to say to girls. But I think a girl who's a

good friend would be different. You could tell her you feel shy sometimes or all the time. Girls seem more understanding than boys."

Beth admits:

"Sometimes I get really, really shy around boys, any boys, even boys that are nice and friendly. Sometimes I'm even shy around my girlfriends. It overcomes me like I'm drowning. Waves and waves of shyness. It's embarrassing because I can't talk and I just become quiet."

Alison reminds everyone:

"Sometimes people don't know you're having a shyness attack. It only seems so to you. Keep on talking and see what they have to say. I've never had anyone say, 'Gee, Alison, you seem shy today. Why don't you get with it?' And you know why nobody says that? Because they probably feel shy, too. That's the real reason."

Eric admits:

"Shy? Of course I'm shy. Unbearably shy. But I stopped being like that in the third grade and

became Eric the Funny. That helped me a lot. Anyone who is shy should be forced to do stand-up comedy. Did you ever see a stand-up comic? I bet half of them were shy kids."

Robyn says honestly:

"Talk about heavy-duty shyness! I didn't even admit I had it for a long time. It comes over me like the flu or something. I hope someday my shyness will go away."

Girls who are shy should adjust to their shyness by admitting it to themselves, and not attempting friendships with boys on whom they have crushes. They should know that shyness doesn't necessarily last forever and that it isn't the worst thing on the planet earth. Whether you are a little shy or very shy, know that other girls and boys are experiencing the same thing.

Asking for Help

There's no reason not to ask for help getting over your shyness. There are counselors, parents, older brothers and sisters, and other friends. Most likely they will tell you about their experiences with shyness, and give you tips on how to beat it or live with it.

Here's how a jury of your peers would advise you to combat shyness.

1. **Stick to small talk** — Don't attempt heavy conversations if you are going through a shy time.

Most girls want to know — what is small talk? Is it only small words as opposed to big words? No. Small talk is what your parents probably have with the neighbors.

"Hi, looks like we're in for a storm tonight."

"Oh, I like your coat. Where did you get it?"

"How's your grandmother? I know you said she was sick."

Do you get the idea? You've seen adults do it millions of times, and maybe you do it, too.

Alison gives good advice:

"Don't be too serious when you're feeling shy. Why? Because no one will notice that you're shy as long as you talk about something."

Beth has her own ideas:

"In a way it's spoiled to be shy. That means the whole world owes you something and you don't have to say anything or do anything. When I feel shy I talk myself out of it and then I'm okay."

Jeremy, who never feels shy, is enviable and someone to imitate:

"I don't know. Nothing is ever that important for me to feel shy over it or anything. I just think everyone likes me and I like everyone, so why not show it?"

2. **Listen** — Maybe the most important thing you can do when you're shy (or even when you're not) is to listen to what the other person has to say, and respond. That way no one will suspect you're shy — they'll think you're polite. You don't have to worry about what you are going to say. Just listen. It's the best trick in the world and one to remember always. Be a good listener.

Beth says:

"It's easier to listen than to talk. And when you listen it goes so much further, don't you think?"

Jessica agrees and disagrees:

"That's okay if the person you are with isn't shy. But if he or she is, you'll feel uncomfortable with neither of you talking! Know when to listen and then listen well."

Eric says:

"I never listen. I always tell jokes and everyone laughs. Sometimes I'd like to know more about the other person."

3. **Be yourself** — This may seem obvious. But the truth is you might seem stiff and unlike yourself because of your shyness. Try very hard to relax and be natural.

Mitchell advises girls:

"You should know that boys are just as shy as girls. So try to act calm as if you were with an old friend."

Debbie confesses:

"I never really feel shy. But I think boys do. Otherwise they would talk more and have something better to say."

Lauren loves to tell this story:

"Once when I was in the fifth grade I liked this boy and I think he liked me back. So I made up this story, telling him I was originally from Mexico. It turns out he has grandparents who

live in Mexico. Boy, did I feel funny. I just wanted to impress him. I guess I just got the wrong boy."

Roger doesn't understand:

"I think when people think you should be yourself it's hard, because you also want to make a good impression. Maybe you could be yourself but fix it up a little."

Robyn reflects:

"I always try to be myself. I think it's easier. Even with other girls, if you put on airs or try to be something you're not, it never works out right. After all, you don't want to be labeled a nerd."

Nerds of the world, arise! Who's calling who a nerd?! What's a nerd? Couldn't that just be a fellow shy person?

Eric admits:

"I was a nerd in the fourth grade. I didn't want to be that, so I changed."

Jessica also admits:

"I don't even know for sure what a nerd is except I always make fun of them, I think, though I know it's not nice. A nerd is someone who just doesn't fit in."

Debbie says honestly:

"You see, frankly, I think that most boys are nerds."

Alison cautions:

"I think you should watch out who's calling whom a nerd. Today's nerd may be tomorrow's friend."

Not only is it cruel and unnecessary to label someone a nerd, it doesn't even make sense. What is a nerd? A nerd is just someone who dares to be different. And actually, that takes a lot of courage! So why should you make fun of a so-called nerd and force him or her to be lonely and set apart?

Richie says:

"I think it's unfair to label other people. For all I know some kids are calling me a nerd right this minute, only not to my face. I guess you should remember that a person you think is a nerd could turn out to be really neat."

6.
Role-Playing

THIS is a simple game to play. It's used in training salespeople and also in acting classes. Girls can play boys, boys can play girls. It's much like improvisation. When you role-play, you make an outline of what you could say to a boy. That lessens your shyness. Start out by practicing with a girlfriend. Let her be a boy and you be a girl. Then ask each other questions:

Q: How did you do on the history quiz?

A: I'm not so sure I did that well. How do you think you did?

Q: Oh, history is my favorite subject. I think I'm going to be a history teacher when I grow up. Would you like some help with your history?

A: That would be great.

Q: Maybe at free time?

A: Maybe then. Though most times I play punchball.

And so on. But if you read between the lines, the person who was asking all the questions was able to steer the role-playing toward what he or she wanted.

Basically the way role-playing works is you go back and forth until the other person has a hard time saying no. Remember that most boys are shy, so this helps them along.

Here's another one:

She: Hi, do you want to play at recess?

He: OK.

She: How about punchball?

He: Yeah.

She: It will be fun.

He: Yeah. I'm looking forward to it.

She: Yeah.

When you're role-playing you make up the scene as you go along. Nothing is rehearsed and nothing is planned. Of course you may explode in laughter, and it might not be as organized as these examples, but it does prepare you for conversations with a boyFRIEND. Try it.

Is It Worth It?

Alison advises:

"Is it worth it to work so hard to get a boyFRIEND? I think it's worth it, and really, it isn't hard work at all. It must be fun to have a boyFRIEND."

Richie advises:

"I think it's great for boys and girls to be friends. So you have to work at it a little. I think it's worth it."

Beth advises:

"I think it's worth it, of course. In fact it's not so much work. I just go up to someone and say, 'Hi, I want to be your friend!' "

Jessica advises:

"Everything that's fun takes a little work. And besides, this is just a little bit of work. I think it's worth it."

7.
Staying Friends After School

MANY girls I talked to said they had boyFRIENDS only in school. None of them called their boyFRIENDS on the phone and talked to them outside of the school or school yard. It just wasn't done.

Eric says:

"I think it's one thing to be friends with a boy or girl in school. It's another thing to call them up."

Beth says:

"I don't think it's necessary to be friends with boys after school. Just during school. I would feel funny hanging around with them after school."

Jeremy says:

"I would be really surprised if a girl called me."

Jessica says:

"I think it would be fun to have boyFRIENDS, but I don't think we would have to get together after school. No one does. It isn't done in our school. I don't know about other places."

Most girls I talked to didn't know why they never saw their boyFRIENDS after school or called them in the evening. It was as if the friendship died off as soon as they left school. To really be friends with boys, why not try talking to them outside of school, too, about homework, or school events, or anything. This will make your friendship even more special.

How to Be Friends with a
GIRL

8.
You Gotta Be Kidding!

RICHIE says:

"Oh, forget it! I might as well pick a Doberman pinscher to be my friend. All girls care about is their clothes and sticking together like glue. It would be wonderful if they weren't so stuck-up. Then you could do it. I would like to do it."

Joey is kind of looking forward to it:

"I used to be a girl-hater. Now I would like to have some friends who are girls. It's just that I don't know how it's done. So I end up believing I still hate girls, when I don't think I really do."

Popular Jeremy likes everybody — even girls. But he doesn't know how to have girl-FRIENDS. So, the boy who *looks* like he has everything doesn't really. Like everyone else, he doesn't understand how boys can be friends with girls and not "like" them.

Eric observes:

"I would like to be friends with girls, but I act like it's a big joke, I guess, because I don't know what I'm doing."

Alison advises:

"I think boys should be friends with girls, but I sometimes think they just don't know how to act around girls."

Mitchell offers:

"I would be afraid to have a girlFRIEND. I'm basically afraid of girls but I don't admit it. How would I act?"

Boys Will Be Boys

As told by Jessica:

"Sometimes they act like real brats. Once me

and a bunch of girls were coming out of school and the boys were waiting with slabs of wet toilet paper to pelt at us. It was totally gross. Like a war — only no one gave us weapons to fight back. They got into trouble. None of us felt we could be friends after that. It was just too immature. Both the fifth- and sixth-graders were in on it.

As told by Alison:

"One day the cafeteria served fresh oranges for a treat. Some of the boys got this bright idea: Pelt the girls with orange slices when they come out of the school. But it backfired, I'm happy to say, because how would you feel if one of your best friends almost broke your glasses? In a boy versus girl situation, some of the girls stayed to fight back. But I was almost the only girl on the school bus. I thought it was disgusting. The boys got detention for a week."

Most boys like girls when they get past the basic misunderstanding of "liking" girls (and pretending they don't). With girlFRIENDS you have friendships and you feel at ease with a girl. You can talk to her in a new way. Not exactly like you do your boyfriends. You can talk to them in a different way, in a friendly way. That's what having a girlFRIEND is for. They're just a little bit different than a boyfriend.

Once they got past "liking" versus liking, most boys enjoyed the difference and the friendliness of not having a crush on a girl but being friends with a girl.

Boys Who Have GirlFRIENDS

Jeremy tells his secret to being popular, even with girls:

> *"I don't even like it, but I have this quality of attracting boys and girls. There's only so much of me to go around. I would say that girls make better friends. They are more sensitive to things and people, and they talk easily."*

Richie remembers a lost friendship:

> *"I had this great friend, Veronica, who I sat next to in school. She helped me once when I was in assembly because I forgot my good shoes and only had my sneakers with my suit. But at lunch she ran all the way to my house and picked up my shoes. I really felt sad when she*

moved. There's been no one I can talk to, really *talk to, since then.*

Jeremy confesses to everyone:

"I guess Beth is my best friend of friends who are girls. I think it's because I don't have much of a crush on her. Debbie tells me how girls feel about things. It's much easier to really *talk to her than to boys who are my friends. I don't know why that is, but it is."*

The strange case of Elise, told by Eric:

"I was friends with Elise at the time. She's in the sixth grade. So she came over, and who should be home but my older brother, who is in the eighth grade. Anyway, she started to come over to be with my older brother. But even after they decided they liked each other, I still had this friendship. She's still friends with me, but she keeps on asking me about my brother."

Girls Give Advice to Boys Who Want to Be Friends

1. **Be yourself —** Don't try to play games or show off. That's just a cover-up and it usually

doesn't impress girls. Especially girls whom you'd like to get to know better. Be yourself and girlFRIENDS will let you be yourself.

Richie says:

"I have trouble getting to know girls. The best idea is to try to be myself. That way I'm not shy!"

Alison advises:

"I think boys are the nicest when they let down all their defenses and just act like themselves. I would advise any boy who wants to have a girlFRIEND to not play any games, cut the wisecracks, and just stop trying to impress people."

2. **Don't give advice unless a girl asks for it** — Boys sometimes think that they were put on this planet to help girls out. Sometimes this is nice, for sure. But other times, giving unasked-for advice as a way of showing friendship to a girl doesn't sit well with her. You could lose the friendship of a girl who doesn't want to be advised.

Jessica shares:

"I can't stand it when boys give advice when I didn't ask for it. How come girls never do it to them? They give advice just because they're boys, and they figure they know more."

Beth says:

"One thing I don't like about boys is when they give advice or tell you what to do or what you should do. I don't know what to say when they start doing that. I wonder if they know how much girls mind that."

3. **Listen when a girl is talking** — Listening is a very important rule in being friends with a girl. If you do all the talking, it will be a one-sided friendship and the girl will quickly lose interest in you.

Debbie lets boys know:

"One thing I don't like about boys is they're such loudmouths. They never listen."

Alison says:

"If there's any one thing I would tell boys to do it's not to get nervous and feel that they have

to do all the talking all of the time. You have to listen to what a girl's saying. Listen and talk. Listen and talk. Not talk, talk, talk."

4. **Give up the wars** — To be friends with girls, obviously, it would help if you gave up the attacks, like the orange slice wars and the wet toilet paper capers. These battles make the girl the enemy, and it's more fun if girls become your friends. This is the name of the game. So drop the warfare and the pranks, and concentrate on knowing girls not as victims but as friends.

Richie admits:

"I used to be into that. Playing tricks on girls. Till I found out it hurt them and no girl would be my friend. It's more fun not to do that."

Jessica says:

"That's the type of boy I positively hate, the kind that plays pranks and messes things up. If a boy wants to be friends with me, he should leave all that behind."

5. **Just be a friend** — Simple to say, you might think, but hard to do. But there it is.

And it's not a hard rule to follow, once you get to know a girl. Just be a friend. It really isn't that mysterious or difficult.

Lauren admits:

"I don't really like boys all that much because I don't trust them but I would like them a lot better if they would just be friendly."

Eric says:

"I would like to be friends with girls and be a friend, but what about all my jokes? Sometimes I turn girls off with my joking, but also that's how I can be a friend. I can make them laugh."

9.
Clamming Up

CLAMMING up comes from the idea of being shut tight as a clam. When boys have this happen to them they might appear much shyer than they actually feel. It often happens to lots of boys, and then they lose control of who they are and what they say.

Mitchell admits to clamming up:

"I feel like a space cadet. I feel like they buzzed me in from another planet. It happens to me all the time. Maybe that's why I'm afraid of girls."

Alison also knows how it feels to clam up and would like to share it with boys:

"With girls it's different. A girl just feels like

she's very shy. For me it's like having peanut butter in my mouth and no glass of milk."

Richie says:

"A lot of times I will clam up. It happens usually when I least expect it. But it happens a lot. Like someone washed my mouth out with soap and water, and I'm afraid if I open it, bubbles will come out."

What do you do when you clam up? It seems like a no-way-out situation when you're stuck in it. But maybe it helps to know that a lot of boys clam up and have the same symptoms. The thing is, when you're in it, it seems like you're trapped in glue. You can't say anything, can't do anything.

How to stop clamming up:

1. **Listen to what she is saying** — Sometimes it doesn't matter if you clam up or not, if the girl is talking. Just listen to what she's saying and respond. No one will ever know, and chances are it will pass.

Beth reveals:

"I really can't tell when a boy is clamming up. I guess I talk too much."

Alison says:

"It wouldn't matter to me if a boy clammed up. I mean, I wouldn't go so far as to label him a nerd. If he couldn't talk he shouldn't feel bad, he just shouldn't talk. I guess I wouldn't care."

2. **Try to be yourself, and as yourself, try to say a few words** — Sometimes when you clam up you can manage a few words that will fake it for a while. Like "How did you do on the test?" or "I like your shirt." Just say a few words to stay in the ball game. Chances are she won't know you've clammed up, and it will make you feel better. Just say *something*. Say anything to break out of being clammed up, and no one will know.

Jessica says:

"I understand how a boy can clam up, and it would be okay with me. As long as he acted like he was interested in the friendship. Otherwise I would think he was snubbing me."

Then there's always the question of cover-ups.

Eric says:

"Everyone has a cover-up. Some people act snobby or like they're above it all. Me, I do a few pranks, crack a few jokes. Everyone laughs. But it's a cover-up."

Alison says:

"I don't know if they're so much cover-ups as shyness breakers. I don't mind if a boyFRIEND has a cover-up as long as it's a nice one."

Stuttering Sufferers

There's no pill you can pop into your mouth. Some boys pretend to clam up so as not to stutter. Some don't know what hit them. Others don't know what to do about it. But there is hope.

Richie is an ex-stutterer:

"I used to stutter back in third grade. I even stutter now when I least expect it. It really makes me angry. Most people won't say anything about it to my face. I would advise anyone to talk slower when you feel you're going to stutter. Don't talk faster. As far as talking about stuttering with other people, I don't talk about it at all. It just makes me feel more shy."

Mitchell remembers:

"There was a time I put pebbles in my mouth to stop stuttering. I thought it would help, but what happened was I got a toothache."

Alison advises:

"I don't think boys, especially *boys, should stop talking when they start to stutter. That way a girl might think they were snobby or didn't want to talk. See, sometimes it's hard to tell if a person is stuttering and not stumbling."*

What is stuttering? Well, even some experts don't really know what it is. It has to do with the mind and the mouth not always coming together because of nervousness and shyness. It's unfair, really, because it makes you more nervous and shy. When you're thinking it will take a year to get out a word like *and*, and you think you'll die of embarrassment until you spit it out, just remember other people don't notice as much as you do. Another thing to keep in mind is that other people don't *care* as much as you do. But they don't know what to say, so it is awkward for them as well. Should you joke about it or refer to it? That's up to you. But the thing to remember is explaining it requires more words to tie up your mouth. The best thing to do is let it pass. A lot of people, children *and* adults, stutter.

What Is Shyness?

Shyness plagues boys differently than it does girls. Sometimes girls can be shy but cover for it. Boys are shy and clam up or feel like they're buzzed in from a different planet. But shyness can ruin a lot of boy/girl friendships by inhibiting or holding back the fun of it.

There are two types of shyness: 1. being totally shy, 2. being shy in certain situations.

Being Totally Shy

You may think there's no hope for you as a totally shy boy — that everyone else will have girls who are girlFRIENDS and you will be left behind, the shyest boy in the class, the shyest boy in the school, the shyest boy in the world. You're not any of these things, of course; it just feels that way.

Being Situationally Shy

This isn't difficult to understand. It just means you are shy in certain situations. For example, you might feel tongue-tied when a girl approaches you, until you get to know her. Or you might get shy in odd situations when you least expect it, and there's no figuring it out.

Take this true-false quiz to see if you're all-over shy or just-in-certain-situations shy:

I am almost always shy.

I don't know anyone more shy than I am.

I am shy some of the time, like at school.

I'm only shy at certain times, but when it happens, I feel *very* shy.

I'm shy around certain kinds of people.

My shyness turns people off.

I feel I'll be shy forever.

If you got over fifty percent true you are situationally shy, not totally shy. That means there's nothing to worry about. Except when you're in those particular situations.

There is something you can do to help get over your shyness. It might seem silly at first, or remind you of an acting class, but you can almost *rehearse* for when shyness overtakes you. The trick is called role-playing and was discussed in the girls' section of this book.

Role-Playing

Grab a friend and play this game together. First, come up with a situation and then act it out, so that when the situation comes up in school with a girl, or even a boy, you can handle it. Salespeople use this trick in their work, so why can't you use it to make friends?

You: Hi. I thought we could play punchball together at recess.

Her: Okay. That would be fun.

Or:

Her: How have you been? I haven't seen you in a few days. Were you sick?

You: Yeah, I had the flu. I missed the math test. Was it bad?"

Her: I think I did okay. I can help you if you want.

You: Yeah, I'd like that. What about at free time?

Her: Okay, I'll bring my math book.

That's role-playing, and you can practice it with friends until you feel comfortable with it. If you're prepared to talk, you won't feel so shy.

10.
Can You Pick the Right Girl?

YOU'RE probably thinking, Oh, no, do I have to work at this? She's just a girlFRIEND. But you can't just pick any girl to be your girl-FRIEND. You have to pick a girlFRIEND who will be sympathetic to your problems, listen, be on the same wavelength.

Joey says:

"It's very important to pick a girl you like."

Alison advises:

"Some boys get burned, I guess, when they pick the wrong girlFRIEND, and she turns out not to be a real friend, and then that gives them the wrong idea. You'll know when you have the right girlFRIEND. She won't act like a

girlfriend with you and play silly games or act like girls do."

So it is important to pick the right girl to be a girlFRIEND, but that doesn't mean you have to turn yourself inside out or that this won't work. Most likely, you will pick whomever you pick and that will be the right girl. Try it and see.

How to Do It

For the time being just forget your shyness and plunge right in. You can go up to a girl and say, "Hi, let's be friends" or you can wait and do it in steps.

Beth says:

"I would understand that because that's how I do it and boys usually say yes because they want to be friends, too."

Jeremy admits:

"I wish a girl would be that straightforward with me instead of beating around the bush. I would like it better and would end up her friend."

Jessica says:

"I think that would be fun if a boy came up to me and did that. I would want to be his friend."

Joey says:

"If a girl did that to me I would say, 'Yes, I want to be friends,' and I'd give it a try."

Doing it in steps — You could come to have a girlFRIEND slowly, in steps, so you don't have to take her by surprise, and you won't get tongue-tied. *Step 1.* Just start talking to her — ask her some questions about herself or find out how she's doing. *Step 2.* Tell her that you want her to be your girlFRIEND.

Joey says:

"If I did it that way and a girl said she would want to be friends, that would be much easier. I'd really like to have some friends who are girls. Some good friends."

Beth admits:

"Well, I'm not so sure I would understand what

was going on, especially since I just walk up and say, 'Hi, want to be my friend?' And boys usually are interested."

Jessica wonders:

"So many boys clam up that I wonder how they can do that at all. But if a boy ever came up to me and just started talking, I would like it a lot. I think it would be fun. I'm not so sure I could figure out if he wanted to be my friend. But if I wanted to be friends with him I would."

More About Picking a Girl

It may be hard for some boys to think this way. It would be easier to daydream that it's going to happen.

Debbie suggests:

"I think boys would be less shy about having girls for friends if they made a list. If one said no, which I bet they wouldn't do, then you could go on to the next one on the list."

Lauren admits:

"Even though I don't like boys, I would be fair

enough to tell a boy that so he wouldn't waste his time with me."

Jeremy says:

"I wonder if that's the same as going up to a boy and saying, 'Gee, I'd like to be your friend.' Girls are funny. Maybe they'd get angry. Anyway, I never had a girlFRIEND, so I just don't know how it's done."

Jessica says:

"I think boys should pick a friend who's like a boy. I don't mean a tomboy, but a girl who's as comfortable to be with as a boy. I think this is what a boy might want. Sort of a boy/girlFRIEND."

Alison advises:

"Don't spend too much time picking out a girl. I don't think it's worth it. Just pick one and see what happens."

Debbie says:

"I don't see what the problem is at all. A boy

should pick a girl his own friends are friendly with, and be friends with her, too."

Richie has mixed emotions:

"I don't think a boy should just walk up to a girl and say, 'Hi, let's be friends,' although if it worked that would be great. I think a boy and girl should become friends just by playing ball or a game in the yard."

Double Checking How to Approach a Girl

Jeremy says:

"I think what happens is: You go to school one day, and you just say to a girl, 'Hi, let's be friends.' And she either gives you a yes or a no. I doubt if a girl would ever say no. At least I never heard of that happening."

Debbie disagrees:

"On second thought, maybe just walking up to a girl and asking her to be your friend isn't the best way to do it. What about all the shy, sensitive girls out there who might like you, but don't know how to show it. Boys should play with girls in group games like punchball or

Dare during free time or recess. Then the boys can figure out who they want to be friends with and why."

Lauren observes:

"That approach — just asking a girl straight out if she wants to be friends — seems so cold. Like you're picking up a hamburger. I don't know what I'd say with that approach. I guess I'd be flattered, though. Like my mom says, you can never have enough friends."

Robyn says:

"Pick a girl who has the same interests and don't be a show-off."

There Are Friendships and . . .
There Are Friendships

There are friendships with girls that may be some of the best friendships you've ever had, and there are friendships that will be slightly less than that. In the second type of friendship people are not quite *good friends*, just *acquaintances*. These are not the friendships you are looking for. You probably have many acquaintances — every girl in the class, some of whom you may have invited to your third-grade birthday party. But real friendships are different. They are deeper. You are on the same wavelength.

Lauren says:

"Look, I really don't like boys, but if I did I would pick a boy who really liked me."

Joey says:

"I think you can tell who's an ordinary friend, and who's a special friend. You want to be friends with the girl who seems a little like you."

Jeremy admits:

"I think a lot of girls like me, and I like them but not in the same way I like an honest girlFRIEND. It's just not the same thing."

Let the Girls Help

Alison comments:

"Just play sports and then try to get closer to her. You can have a whole conversation by the time there's a good volleyball game going."

Debbie says:

"I would be so happy if a boy came up to me, shook hands, and said, 'I'd like to be your friend.' That would be just great."

Beth agrees:

"I think it's just great to walk up to a girl and say you want to be her friend. That's what I do and it works every time."

Let the Boys Help

Richie remarks:

"It isn't as if you 'like' the girl. It's just a girlFRIEND. If you've got one picked out, just be friends with her."

Jeremy says:

"My advice would be to go for it. Just ask the girl if you can be friends. She'll probably say yes."

Eric advises:

"Why be so serious about it? Crack a couple of

jokes and see if she wants to be your friend."

Roger says:

"I think you just have to make a move, however you do it. And you can't put it off."

11.
How to Talk to a Girl

ALISON suggests:

"Talk to a girl as you would talk to a boy and then see what happens."

Debbie disagrees:

"Girls are different from boys. If you have a girl who is a friend, you talk about other things. Sometimes you have to talk to a girl like she is a girl. That's what this whole thing is about. Girls don't always talk about sports, for example."

Robyn says:

"How can a girl be friends with a boy just

because he asks her? You have to do a little more than that."

Basically, you talk to girls just the way you talk to your friends who are boys, though you may not discuss sports so much. You can talk about anything to girls — homework, problems, the latest gossip, anything.

Summary

1. Just go up and say, "Hi, I'd like you to be my friend." But somehow say it so it doesn't resemble getting votes for the school election. Do it naturally.
2. Find her in the school yard or after school when you're playing ball, and just start talking.
3. Put friendship first. Then they'll know you don't have a crush on them. Keep the emphasis on friendship.

Houses are built brick by brick, and so are good friendships between boys and girls. Though most boys and girls report they don't talk on the phone, ask yourself, "Why not?" It's only a friend.

Let's take time out to discuss what a lot of boys and girls *don't* do.

Beth says:

"I have one boyFRIEND but we don't talk on the phone. No one I know does. I don't know why."

Jeremy admits:

"I wouldn't know what to say to a girl on the phone. No one in our class calls each other. We just see each other at school."

Jessica says:

"In a way, I wish girls called boys and boys called girls because I think there would be more friendship. I think it would be fun but I'm afraid to call first."

For some reason most of the boys and girls interviewed don't call their girlFRIENDS or boyFRIENDS at all, either after school or on the weekends.

The Story of Peter

Karin was good friends with Peter, but though he lived nearby she never called him or went over to his house after school. One day he was missing from school. Then he was out for a week. She rode her bike over to his house, and no one was home. Then she talked to the neighbors and found out that Peter's dad had died suddenly, and the whole family had packed up and moved to Arizona.

Karin never saw Peter again. He never called her, and she never called him. But she could have been a real friend to him when he really needed one.

It's a mistake not to call your girlFRIEND. Even if you call only occasionally, that's okay. She might be absent from school and you might want to talk to her. Call your girl-FRIENDS, just as girls should call their boyFRIENDS.

Which brings us to an important point — HOW NOT TO BE A FRIEND:

Richie is worried:

"How could I help someone with their problems? I don't even know how to solve mine. It would be better if we didn't talk about those things."

But, after all, who's talking about *solving* problems? All we're talking about is being friends, and being a good listener.

Sometimes boys feel just because they are friends with a girl they should be giving lots of advice. It's not necessary unless a girl asks you for advice. Then you could give it freely.

Debbie says:

"I usually like to get advice from a boy — but only when I ask for it. If no one asks for it it's usually wrong to give advice or, at least the advice is hard to take."

Jessica says flat out:

"I would tell him right away that I don't need his advice unless I ask for it."

Robyn says:

"He might be pressing his luck."

As bad as too much advice is when a boyFRIEND confides in his girlFRIEND too much.

Eric admits:

"If I had a girlFRIEND I would tell her all my problems."

Many boys are brought up with the same idea:

1. That it's their duty to give advice to girls they are close to.

2. That they have to tell all their problems to their girlFRIEND — that's what she's there for.

Neither is what friendship is for. Too much advice, or too much talk about your problems, and more than a few girls said you might be pressing your luck.

Messing Up a Relationship

How can a boy mess up a relationship? Easy.

Eric asks:

"If they stop doing magic tricks?"

Joey says:

"I think it's girls who would mess it up. They might try flirting with you or they might start acting different. Girls are always changing."

Alison observes:

"I don't think boys would start out to mess it up. But I think they might do it by accident and then be sorry."

What boys might do is act too aggressive and tough, trying to show off around girls. Do you know what that's called? It's macho. You must always curb your tendency to be macho around girls with whom you want to become friends.

Some girls and boys didn't really know what macho means. They responded this way:

A. Is it a Mexican dish?

B. Is it Spanish for "matches"?

C. A new pet?

D. None of the above.

Girls interpret being macho in different ways.

Debbie says:

"Being macho is poor behavior for a boy. Lots of boys are macho. What matters is how they let it affect your friendship."

Alison adds:

"It's just a cover-up, a lot of bluster, which a boy thinks is good for his girlFRIENDS. If they can stand it!"

Why Do Boys Act Macho?

Acting macho is a boy's way of showing his pride, and is sometimes even a put-down of girls. Sometimes he learns this from older brothers, sometimes from his father, oftentimes from boyfriends. He likes to call the shots.

But if you have a girlFRIEND — things are different. You can be open and honest and you don't have to hide behind a macho attitude.

12.
Peer Pressure Explored

PEER pressure — it's something most people don't understand. It's when your boyfriends think you are paying too much attention to your friend who is a girl, and not spending enough time with them. It's mostly the girl's fault as you'll begin to see.

Jeremy says:

"I've never had that happen to me, but I know other guys have. First they leave him out of one football game, and then another. Until that boy asks why, and they tell him what the matter is."

Eric recalls:

"That happened to me. One of my best buddies

had a girlFRIEND and he wasn't spending enough time with us. We were eating lunch, and when this boy went to get a glass of milk, we opened up his sandwich and put in hot peppers. When he bit into that sandwich, it was the funniest thing you ever saw. And he got the message."

Alison says:

"Boys should ignore other boys if they want to have a friendship with a girl. Don't let them tell you what to do."

Jessica says:

"I don't know why boys do that. I think they do that more than girls. If my girlfriends tried to stop me from having boys who were friends or spending time with them, I would really be angry."

Maybe it would be time to put a stop to pranks and jokes and see what the stakes are. Why should you have to give up a friendship for the sake of your boyfriends? PEER PRESSURE can be heavy but don't give in to it.

Stand up for what you want to do.

Striking Deals

Roger says:

"I might agree to spend five afternoons a week with my boyfriends but spend lunchtime with my girlFRIEND."

Mitchell says:

"I'm so shy I can't think of that situation happening. But if it did, I would just tell my boyfriends to back off."

Alison says:

"I think there could be a trade-off. Maybe the boy could see his girlFRIEND, like, at free time, and maybe see his friends after school. Then he could be with both of them."

Beth admits:

"I think I've done that to a girlfriend who broke away from the group and found a boy who was a friend. We just took her aside and said, 'You can't do this anymore.' And she said, 'Oh yes

I can. I have a right to have other friends.' And then she struck up a deal with us. Sometimes she would see her best girlfriends and sometimes she would see him."

And then, as if that isn't enough, here comes the peer pressure from your family.

"Did you hear? Richie's got himself a little girlfriend."

And soon all your relatives and family are on your back with the same playful chant — "Richie's got a girlfriend, Richie's got a girlfriend." You protest, "She's not a girlfriend." Grandma giggles and says, "She's a girl and a friend, isn't she?"

And what can you say???

You could explain the truth to them. That you have a friend who is a girl. That you don't have a crush on her. That she even "likes" someone else. That you just talk in school and have the same interests. You could explain all that and see what happens.

Joey says:

"I think if it ever happened to me I would just

tell them the truth. But I don't think they want to hear that. For some reason, they want to think I like *someone.*"

Beth admits:

"If I ever had that kind of pressure from my family, I would say something. But I don't think it would do any good. They would just think it was too cute."

Jeremy says:

"That's not really peer pressure. That's pressure. I think if I told them what was going on they would stop teasing me. Maybe."

Then there is the problem of the peer pressure coming from *her* friends.

Alison says:

"I think you have to give her some support so that she will know how to deal with her girlfriends and you can keep her as a girlFRIEND. Tell her how you can help her."

Beth says:

"I think the best way a boy can help a girl in that situation is to let her do what's best."

Eric admits:

"Actually you can't joke around about that. The boy should help the girl or she won't have any girlfriends."

Jessica says:

"You just have to be diplomatic. It's not the end of the world. He should just talk over what's happening with her girlfriends."

13.
How to Meet Girls

MANY of the girls and boys reported that they played ball together — baseball, football, punchball — and it was a shared activity. That is, in fact, where many girls decide to become friends with boys.

Sunday school friends — Sunday school friends come in all sizes and shapes. You might meet them every week in Sunday school or in your church or synagogue. These friendships are safe friendships. You only see them once a week and you might not have much in common except that you like each other. You go to different schools, yet you still have stuff to talk about. This is one way to find a very nice girlFRIEND, one you would see every week.

Drama group — To anyone who's ever been in a play at school or somewhere else, the informal rehearsals and the fact that you can talk backstage when you're not acting onstage make this a fabulous chance to meet a girlFRIEND. Also, there's something that frees you up when you're playing another person. It's like role-playing. Try being in a play and you may meet a girl who's a perfect friend. If you are shy, a play can take away all your worries.

Have your bike ready to go — Bike to the park, bike to a girl's house, use your bike to meet people. If other people bike-ride, this can be a shared activity, and you can meet girls and possibly a girlFRIEND. You can even drop by at someone's house and get to know her better.

Summer camp — This is a way many boys and girls meet. Their relationships may only last for a summer, but they are good friendships.

Alison says:

> *"I went to camp. One night the boys put bugs in our beds. I didn't like camp, but I was friends with* some *of the boys that I remember as being nice."*

Richie comments:

"I went to camp last summer and I met this girl, Annie. We hit it off real well and were friends. Camp was different from school, where I'm shy. Now we're pen pals."

Beth says:

"At camp last summer I met this boy, Billie, and we were friends and had a good time together. At the end of the summer we had to say good-bye because he lives upstate. Now we can just be pen pals."

The fact is, you can *meet* girls all over.

Here's a list of some of the other places where you can meet girls:

The library
The corner store
Swimming, tennis, and music lessons
Down the block
4H, depending on where you live

The list goes on and on, but most of all, you can meet girls in school. And that leads us to still another sort of pressure . . . being competitive with girls in sports.

Richie confesses:

"I always have to win. I never thought about that kind of pressure. Truth is, I would try to mess up the score so I could win."

Jeremy says:

"Sometimes I don't think girls should be included in sports. My father doesn't like us to have girls in our games. He always says, 'What if the girl gets hurt?' "

Jessica disagrees:

"In that way, I think boys are off the wall. Just wait. More and more girls are playing with boys in boys' sports. If they want girls as friends, they should realize that girls want to play sports, too."

If you start being too competitive, girls may reject you. But they may reject you in other ways, too. Sometimes the rejection is imagined. But often it's real. What do you do if the girl whom you want to be your girlFRIEND rejects you?

14.
Rejecting Rejection

So what if you walk up to some girl and say, "Hi, I'd like to be your friend." Chances are she'll say yes. But what if she doesn't? Then you've been rejected, and you have to deal with it.

Joey says sincerely:

"I wouldn't dwell on it. Maybe because in this situation it's not a real rejection."

Richie admits:

"I guess I would cover up by doing something to hide the hurt. Maybe I would be angry, or play tricks on people."

Eric comments:

"That's how most of my better jokes begin. They begin when I'm hurt. I can shake anything just by being the life of the party."

Now let's hear it from the girls and what they do when they reject a boy who wants to be friends.

Jessica admits:

"I rejected two boys whom I didn't think would be fun mainly because I knew each one of them had a crush on me. So they didn't act normal. They said, 'Hi, want to be friends?' But I knew they had something else in mind. They wanted to be boyfriend-girlfriend, so I just said, 'No thanks.' "

Debbie says:

"I've never rejected a boy yet, but I would. But I would do it nicely so they wouldn't get hurt. I hate it when I'm rejected."

Robyn shares:

"I've been rejected plenty of times. If I were rejecting someone I'd do it gently so that the boy wouldn't feel bad."

How to Reject Rejection

Let's say you plan on asking a special girl to play punchball or do something else, and she says, "No thanks," for whatever reason. Do you ask her the reason? Do you take no for an answer? How do you deal with your feelings when she rejects you? Rejections can hurt. If you try to ignore it or pretend it doesn't exist, that's even worse. If you try to crack jokes and cover it over, you'll end up hurting even more.

Alison says:

"Maybe she's got all the signals wrong. Maybe she thinks you want to be her boyfriend and she's not ready. It might be a mix-up. Maybe you shouldn't give up."

Beth remarks:

"I wouldn't let it hurt you. There are so many rejections in life. You try out for the school play and you don't make it. You lose the spelling bee. I would just pick another girl and chalk it up to the fact that the first one didn't understand."

Richie says:

"I can't stand the thought of rejection. I would rather just meet a girl playing a game or sports or something. That way you know how she feels about you."

Seeing Rejection for What It Is

No one likes rejection. But it may not really be a rejection. Maybe the girl didn't understand. Maybe she couldn't handle it. There are a thousand *maybe*'s but it isn't worth asking yourself, "What's wrong with me?"

Alison says:

"Maybe you should ask her why she rejected you. That way you would really know there was nothing wrong with you."

Beth advises:

"Don't take it too seriously. Find out why she rejected you. Because when you think about it, that's odd. It's not as if you have bad breath or anything. All you did was ask to be her friend."

Never Take No for an Answer

Don't get set up for a rejection. And don't

take no for an answer. If she just doesn't want to be friends with you, you can't force her to. But you should try to find out why she said no.

Eric says:

"That would be the kind of thing that would happen to me. All I want to do is be friends with the girl and she doesn't like me."

Be More Aggressive

Will you still get rejected? Being more aggressive means your girlFRIEND will know exactly what you mean when you ask her and it won't be misinterpreted.

Joey admits:

"I guess that's the best way to do it. Let everyone know from the start what you are going to do so when you do it you don't get rejected."

Jessica says:

"I think you might still get rejected, but you've made yourself clear and you don't have to feel so shy and hurt if a girl just happens to say no to you."

Mitchell disagrees:

"I don't think acting like you know what you're doing means you won't get rejected. I would feel terrible if I picked out a girl and she decided to reject me."

How to Be Successful

Actually there are no rules on how to be successful in getting a girlFRIEND. But it does help to know how a good friendship between a boy and a girl works.

Joey says:

"I think the way to be successful is to really like and respect the girl. That way she's probably already friends with you."

Debbie says:

"I don't think you should look at it as successful or unsuccessful. You should just make friends with the girl so that when you ask her to be your girlFRIEND she automatically will be."

How Not to Be Successful

Don't act like you own the relationship.

Don't tell her what to do. Don't give her unasked-for advice. Don't be bossy. Just be a good friend.

Alison advises:

"No one likes a show-off and no one likes a boy who tells people what to do. Just because you're a boy doesn't mean you can give advice or tell a girl who's a friend what to do."

Jeremy says:

"I hope I don't fall into that trap. I tend to boss my cousins and sisters around. I think you do that more with girls you 'like.' "

Richie admits:

"I do give girls advice. I have a younger sister who doesn't know what she's doing and I give her advice all the time. Maybe I should remember not to."

Joey says:

"When I'm with a girl I get nervous and I talk about myself all the time. Somehow I guess I better watch that."

After the How To's of having a friendship with a girl come the What If's. For instance:

What If She Thinks I Like Her?

Alison says:

"The thing to do since it's not a crush relationship is just talk it over with her. Maybe she doesn't like you. Maybe it's your imagination. But if you're friends you should say something like, 'Hey, do you like *me?' and then if she says no, you'll know, and if she says yes, you can talk it over and maybe talk her out of it. Not every girl will like you."*

Roger says:

"I guess that could happen sometimes when you least expect it. It could happen to the boy, too. Probably what you should do is talk it over so you don't ruin the friendship."

Debbie admits:

"Well, that really makes me mad when boys think that way. What if she doesn't like him and he's just reading into things? I can see that might happen, but I don't think it's that

type of relationship. Yep, that really makes me mad."

It may be that your macho attitude is showing more than you think, and that *you* can't handle a relationship with a girl. If you ask her, you might find out that she doesn't "like" you at all, and you have entirely the wrong impression. Talk with your friend and you'll get the truth.

Beth says:

"Acting macho is just the kind of behavior I don't like in boys, no matter how it shows. Boys should do something about it before they intend to have friendships with girls."

Jeremy informs us:

"The first time I found out about boys being macho, I thought it was a disease. But now that I know about it, I can think first before I act. I thought I was born feeling like I had to be macho, but then I found out that's what happens to boys along the way."

Joey says:

"Sometimes I feel funny being a boy. I'm just a normal boy — what did I do? Now they tell me I'm acting macho? Maybe girls are acting some way, too."

Richie admits:

"I've heard of 'macho' but I thought older boys acted that way. I don't really know how to stop it since I don't really know when I'm doing it."

What If She Thinks I'm Weird?

This is based on: What if I don't think I'm good enough? But you have to realize that if there's a friendship, you *are* good enough. To begin with, you both like each other and it may prove to be the best friendship you've ever had. So keep in mind she won't think you're weird and even if you are, maybe that's what she likes about you.

What If It Doesn't Work Out?

If it's not working out, you do the same thing you would if you thought she liked you. You talk things over. If it still doesn't work — OK, it doesn't work, but don't build it up in your imagination. The reality is you're still friends, although maybe not best friends. Usually it will work out. Girls need boys to be friends with and boys need girls to be friends with.

Eric complains:

"No one takes me seriously. One time this girl got mad at me and said my jokes weren't funny. I didn't want to be friends with her. I don't know how I'll be able to be friends with girls. I feel more comfortable around boys. It's hard."

Joey agrees it's not easy:

"I try to make friends with girls but it seems they don't want to make friends with me. When I'm goofing around they laugh, but I can't get close to them. Maybe I wasn't meant to have girlFRIENDS. I'm not having any luck."

Mitchell bows out:

"I can't take the time to be friends with girls, because every day after school I help my dad in the store. So what's the sense in wasting my time if I can't spend enough time at it?"

None of these excuses, which is what they are, makes any sense. Eric had one bad experience. Joey might make it too hard for himself, and Mitchell is ignoring his in-school time to make friends with girls. If a boy doesn't want to be friends with a girl, if he just wants to stick to his boyfriends, that's fine. But excuses just won't do.

What Do Girls Think of All This?

Many girls want to be friendly with a particular boy. Some don't, but most want boyFRIENDS. Basically they like boys. It's not as hard as you think to have a girlFRIEND, because they want friends who are boys. They're just as afraid of you as you are of them. They're afraid of rejection, of doing it wrong, of messing it up. The funny thing about girls and boys is they have differences, but they are not so different.

Alison repeats:

"I want a boyFRIEND. There are two boys I'd like to be friends with in my class. I just have to ask them, but I'm afraid they'll say no. I keep putting it off. I wonder sometimes if boys do the same thing. I'm afraid of rejection but I don't really think I'll get one."

Beth has no problems:

I don't see why you have to be shy. Can you imagine a boy saying no to wanting to be friends? What's the big deal about wanting to be friends? If he said no I'd wonder about him. I really would."

So you see, there are girls who want to be your friend. Take the first step and ask them if they want to be your friend. It may be the best friendship you'll ever have. Being friends with a girl is a little different than being friends with another boy, but it's a difference you're going to like.